GIRLZ ROCK!

Escalator Escapade

Holly Smith Dinbergs

illustrated by

Chantal Stewart

MONDO

First published in 2006 by
MACMILLAN EDUCATION AUSTRALIA PTY LTD
627 Chapel Street, South Yarra, Australia 3141

This edition first published in the United States of America
in 2006 by MONDO Publishing.

For information contact:
MONDO Publishing
980 Avenue of the Americas
New York, NY 10018

Visit our web site at http://www.mondopub.com

06 07 08 09 10   9 8 7 6 5 4 3 2 1

ISBN 1-59336-934-4 (PB)

Series created by Felice Arena and Phil Kettle
Project Management by Limelight Press Pty Ltd
Cover and text design by Lore Foye
Illustrations by Chantal Stewart

Printed in Hong Kong

GiRLZROCK!
Contents

Sophie   *Jess*

CHAPTER 1

Runaway Ring

Jess and Sophie are at the mall. They are looking around while Jess's mom gets her hair done.

Jess "See ya later, Mom. Don't worry, we won't get into trouble. I promise!"

Sophie "So your mom thinks we're gonna get into trouble?"

Jess (shrugging) "Well, remember the last time we were here when we pretended to be spies?"

Sophie "Yeah. That security guard freaked out."

Jess "Mmm...he sure got mad when he couldn't find us!"

Sophie "That was so funny."

Jess "Mom didn't think so.

   She was mad at me for days."

The girls stop in front of a jewelry cart.

Jess "Ooh, look! Silver rings. Cool, I love these!"

Jess tries a ring on every finger. She stretches out her fingers to admire the jewelry.

Jess "Who do I remind you of?"
Sophie "Huh?"
Jess "Think 'crystal ball.'"

Jess waves her hands over an imaginary crystal ball and smiles mysteriously.

Sophie "You mean the fortune-teller from the carnival?"

Jess "Yup!"

Sophie "Now all you need is a scarf and some big earrings, and the crowd'll be lining up."

The lady working at the jewelry cart frowns at the girls.

Sophie (whispering) "That lady looks really annoyed."

Jess "What's her problem?"

Sophie "I guess we're not supposed to touch this stuff unless we're gonna buy it."

Jess (shrugging) "That's so not fair! You've gotta try on shoes before you buy 'em. It's the same with rings."

Sophie "Hey, now that you mention it, c'mon. Let's go try on shoes."

Jess "Yeah, great idea, Soph. More shoes—just what you need."

Jess removes the rings, one by one, but she has trouble getting the last one off.

Jess "Oh, no, this one's stuck. Help!"

Jess puts out her hand and Sophie tugs hard on the ring. No luck.

Jess "Owww."
Sophie "You want it off, don't ya?"

Sophie pulls so hard that the ring flies off Jess's finger and onto the escalator. Before the girls know it, the ring is heading to the upper level of the shopping mall.

Sophie "Sorry about that, lady. We'll get it back. C'mon, Jess."

The girls race to the escalator.

CHAPTER 2

Excuse Me

The jewelry-cart lady calls the security guard, who runs over.

Sophie "Jess, quick, get on."

The girls jump onto the bottom step of the escalator, almost crashing into a man and little boy, who step on right in front of them.

Sophie "We'd better get that ring back or we're gonna have to pay for it."

Jess "But it was an accident."

Sophie "I don't think *she* thinks so."

Jess "We've gotta find that ring! Can you see it anywhere?"

Sophie "No, I can't see anything. We've gotta get higher up."

The girls try to move up the escalator, closer to where the ring landed, but they are blocked by the man and boy in front.

Sophie "Excuse me."
Jess (repeating) "Excuse me."

12

The man doesn't hear them, but
the little boy turns and stares.

Sophie (whispering) "We can't wait
for them to go first, Jess. We've got
to get that ring."

Jess "Try saying it again."

Sophie leans forward to the man
in front.

Sophie (loudly) "Excuse me. We've
got to get past. It's an emergency!"

The girls push past, sending the
man and the little boy flying.

Sophie "Sorry, mister!"

Jess "Soph, do you see it? What if the ring gets sucked inside?"

Sophie stares hard at the escalator steps. She just *has* to find the ring.

Sophie (worried) "Everything looks so silvery. I can't make it out."

Jess "Hurry, we're almost at the top."

Sophie "I still don't see it."
Jess "There! There it is! Look!"

Jess points in front. The steps
begin to flatten out ahead of Sophie.
There's not much time left.

Sophie "Yeah! I see it!"

She reaches out to grab the ring.

CHAPTER 3

Mission Accomplished

Sophie sweeps up the ring in her hand just as it's about to disappear through the slot at the top of the escalator.

Sophie "Got it!"
Jess "Phew! For a minute I thought you were gonna have to pay for it."

Sophie "Me pay for it? You're the one with the humongous finger."

Jess "My finger's not big! That ring was too small, that's all."

Sophie "Thank goodness I got the ring or we'd both be in trouble by now."

Jess "But it really wasn't my fault."

Sophie "Yeah, yeah. C'mon. Let's go and give it back while we've still got it. Then we can get to the shoes."

Jess "You and your shoes. You'd think you owned half a shoe company the way you are obsessed with 'em. I'm kinda hungry. Let's go to the food court first."

Sophie "Is there ever any time when you're not hungry?"

The girls step back onto the escalator.
Sophie's shoelace is trailing behind her.

Jess "I think there's someone
waiting down there for us."
Sophie "Oh, no."
Jess "What do you mean? Who is it?"

Sophie "Isn't that the same security guard who chased us around last time?"

Jess squints at the guard.

Jess "Yup, you're right. He won't be happy to see us again."

Sophie "But this was an accident. The ring was lost and we found it. We should get a reward."

Jess "Yeah, right. As if that lady's gonna give us a reward."

The girls approach the bottom of the escalator. As the steps start to flatten out, Sophie tries to move forward.

Sophie (shouting) "Hey, Jess! Help!"

CHAPTER 4

Seriously Stuck

Sophie tries to get Jess's attention,
She calls out again, more loudly this
time.

Sophie "Help! I'm stuck!"
Jess "What do you mean 'stuck?'"
Sophie (louder still) "I can't move my
    foot!"

Jess "What do you mean you can't move your foot?"

Sophie (upset) "Why are you repeating everything I say? Can't you see? I'm stuck. I can't move my foot!"

Jess "What's that string?"

Sophie "That's it! It's my shoelace, it's caught. I'm gonna get sucked into the escalator. Help!"

Jess pulls hard on Sophie's leg to try to release the shoelace, but it won't loosen. Sophie becomes more and more panicked the closer she gets to the bottom.

Jess "Kick it off!"
Sophie "I tried."
Jess "Well, try harder."
Sophie "I can't. It's too tight. Help!"

The security guard notices that Sophie is in trouble. He sees the caught shoelace and immediately pushes the emergency button.

Sophie "Phew ! Thanks mister. Just in time!"

CHAPTER 5

Fries and Laces

There's a loud grinding sound as the escalator comes to a stop. The security guard gets out his pocket knife and cuts the shoelace free.

Jess "Oh, Soph, are you okay? Gee, that was close!"

Sophie "Phew, I'll say! What would have happened if I'd been sucked into the escalator?"

Jess "I dunno. You might've been mince meat. Y'know, perfect for a Sophie-burger!"

Sophie "Oh, that's gross. Funny... but gross."

Jess "At least you can give back the ring now."

Sophie looks puzzled.

Sophie "Me? But I gave it to you."
Jess "What?"
Sophie "The ring. I gave it to you."
Jess "Nuh-uh!"

The jewelry-cart lady and the security guard are standing together, glaring at the girls.

Jess "Sophie, I don't have it."

Sophie (laughing) "Gotcha! Relax. Just kidding. I have it."

Jess "You...! Anyway, you'd better give it back to the lady."

Sophie "Here you are, here's your ring back. We're sorry."

The security guard opens his mouth to say something to the girls just as Jess's mom comes out of the hairdresser.

Jess (overacting) "Mom! Your hair looks really great. Best you've ever had! Can we eat lunch now? I'm starving!"

Sophie "Sounds like a plan."

Jess "Let's eat at Burger Spot. They have really great fries there."

Jess leads her mom toward a takeout food place at the other end of the mall, as far away from the security guard as they can get.

Jess "I love Burger Spot. I think I'll
have a...um...a Sophie-burger...I
mean a hamburger!"

Sophie rolls her eyes, as Jess's
mom asks them what they've been
up to.

Jess "Long story, Mom. But first,
can we buy Sophie some shoelaces?
I think she needs a new pair."

GIRLZ ROCK!
Escalator Lingo

Jess

Sophie

conveyor belt A flexible belt that moves things from one place to another using wheels. It moves the steps of an escalator up or down.

emergency button A button you can push to stop the escalator—but only if there's a real emergency (like if someone gets their shoelace stuck).

escapade A wacky adventure.

handrail The thick rubber belt that you hold on to when you ride the escalator to make sure you don't fall over.

security guard A person who is hired by a place of business to make sure nothing gets stolen.

GIRLZROCK!
Escalator Musts

☆ Don't let anything drag (like a long scarf or untied shoelaces) when you ride an escalator. If it gets caught, you might turn into mince meat!

☆ Treat escalators the same way you would a moving bus. They are both about six tons of moving machinery!

☆ If you have (or see) an emergency and need to stop the escalator, yell "Stop the escalator!" in a loud voice and push the emergency button.

☆ Never, ever push the emergency button on an escalator unless it's really an emergency.

☆ Never try to walk up the "down" escalator, or down the "up" escalator. Your brain will get confused and you'll probably fall over!

☆ If you've pigged out on pizza or ice cream, forget the escalator and take the stairs.

☆ Keep to the right if you are standing on an escalator. Then people who are in a hurry are free to walk on the left side.

GiRLZ ROCK!
Escalator Instant Info

The word "escalator" was created by combining the word *scala*—Latin for "steps"—with the word "elevator."

Escalators are faster than elevators for short distances. Also, a lot more people can be moved quickly on escalators.

The first escalator-like machine was actually a ride at an amusement park! In 1897, Jesse Reno created a new ride—a moving stairway that angled up—at Coney Island in New York.

The world's longest escalator system (a bunch of connected escalators) is in Hong Kong. It's 2,625 feet (800 meters) long and moves 36,000 people a day.

The world's shortest escalator is in a shopping mall in Japan. This escalator is only 2 feet 8 inches (83.4 centimeters) tall.

The longest single escalator is in a Washington D.C. Metro station. The escalator is 508 feet (155 meters) long and it takes almost 3.5 minutes for a rider to go up or down.

GIRLZ ROCK!
Think Tank

1 Who does Jess think she looks like with silver rings on all her fingers?

2 Where does the ring land after Sophie pulls it off Jess's finger?

3 Who frees Sophie when she's stuck on the escalator? How?

4 What type of belt helps the steps of an escalator move up or down?

5 If you see someone get stuck on an escalator, what should you do?

6 Do you think it's a good idea that Jess and Sophie go off on their own when they get to the mall? Why or why not?

7 Why should you never push an escalator's emergency button unless it's a real emergency?

8 What do you think would've happened if Sophie hadn't been freed from the escalator?

Answers

8 Answers will vary.

7 Answers will vary.

6 Answers will vary.

5 If you see someone get stuck on an escalator, yell "Stop the escalator," and push the emergency button.

4 A conveyor belt helps the steps of an escalator move up or down.

3 The security guard frees Sophie by pushing the emergency button and cutting her stuck shoelace.

2 The ring ends up on the escalator going up to the mall's second floor.

1 Jess thinks she looks like the fortune-teller at the carnival.

How did you score?

- If you got most of the answers correct, you should study engineering and become an escalator designer someday.

- If you got more than half of the answers correct, make sure you hold on to the handrail extra tightly whenever you go on an escalator.

- If you got less than half of the answers correct, you'd better stay away from escalators and take the stairs instead!

Hey, Girls!

I love to read and hope you do, too! The first book I really loved was a book called "Mary Poppins." It was full of magic (way before Harry Potter) and it got me hooked on reading. I went to the library every Saturday and left with a pile of books so heavy I could hardly carry them!

Here are some ideas about how you can make "Escalator Escapade" even more fun. At school, you and your friends can be actors and put on this story as a play. To bring the story to life, you can use props such as a silver ring, stairs for an escalator, or shoes with laces trailing behind.

Who will be Sophie? Who will be Jess? Who will be the narrator? (That's the person who reads the parts between Sophie or Jess saying something.) Once you've decided on these details, you're ready to act out the story in front of the class. I bet everyone will clap when you are finished! Hey, a talent scout from a television station might just be watching!

See if someone at home will read this story out loud with you. Reading at home is important and a lot of fun as well.

You know what my dad used to tell me? Readers are leaders!

And remember, Girlz Rock!

Holly Smith Duberg

GIRLZROCK!
When We Were Kids

Holly

Shey

Holly talked to Shey, another *Girlz Rock!* author.

Shey "Did they have escalators when you were little?"

Holly "Very funny. I'm not that old!"

Shey "Just kidding. Did you ever have a problem with an escalator?"

Holly "Not me, but my best friend did. We were yakking and her shoelace really did get caught."

Shey "Was she okay?"

Holly "Yeah. Her dad pulled really hard, and her shoelace broke."

Shey "Does she still have the shoes?"

Holly "No, now she only wears shoes without laces!"

GIRLZ ROCK!
What a Laugh!

Q Why did the ghost go up the escalator?

A To raise its spirits.